THE FABER BOOK

OF CAROLS

and Christmas Songs

THE

FABER BOOK OF CAROLS

and Christmas Songs

Selected and arranged by

ERIC ROSEBERRY

faber and faber

LONDON · BOSTON

First published in 1969
by Faber and Faber Limited
in association with Faber Music Limited
First published in Faber Paperbacks in 1983
by Faber and Faber Limited
3 Queen Square London WC1N 3AU
Printed in Great Britain by
Redwood Burn Ltd
Trowbridge Wiltshire
All rights reserved

Library of Congress Data has been applied for.

British Library Cataloguing in Publication Data

The Faber book of carols and Christmas songs.
1. Carols, English
I. Roseberry, Eric
783.6'552   M1738
ISBN 0–571–13189–1

ACKNOWLEDGEMENTS

Grateful acknowledgements are made to the following
for permission to use copyright material: Percy Dearmer
and Oxford University Press for the words of *Cradle song,
Rocking, Unto us a boy is born, Patapan, Puer natus, Greensleeves* and *Wassail, all over the town* from the *Oxford Book
of Carols*; K. W. Simpson and H. Freeman & Co. for the
words of *What is this fragrance?, He is born* and *Noël! A
new Noël!*; E. M. G. Reed and Evans Brothers Ltd. for
the words of *Infant holy, Infant lowly*; Maurice F. Bell and
Oxford University Press for the words of *Bethlehem*;
Schmitt, Hall & McCreary Company for the words of
Suo-gân, Hark to the angels and *Angels and shepherds* from
Christmas—Its Carols, Customs and Legends; John A.
Parkinson and Oxford University Press for the words of
The boys' carol; Miss Jacubickova and Oxford University
Press for the melody of *Rocking*; R. Vaughan Williams
and Oxford University Press for the melody of *Wassail,
all over the town*; Cecil J. Sharp and Novello & Co. Ltd.
for *The holly and the ivy*; The Royal Musical Association
for *There is no rose, Nova, nova,* and *Hail, Mary, full of
grace*; the Rev. S. Baring Gould and H. Freeman & Co.
for *The angel Gabriel* and *Sleep, my Saviour, sleep.* Acknow-
ledgement is also made to H. Freeman & Co. for the
words of *The shepherds went their hasty way, The Babe in
Bethl'em's manger, The moon shines bright, Our blessèd
Lady's lullaby* and *The seven joys of Mary.*

Every effort has been made to trace copyright owners
and apologies are offered should any copyright have
been unwittingly infringed.

E.R.

PREFACE

In making this choice of Christmas carols I have tried to indicate, in the arrangements, a fresh and unsophisticated approach. Generally speaking, the aim has been to keep the tunes buoyant and rhythmical by means of such pagan devices as ostinato, non-cadential harmony and a dissonance-level that perhaps goes slightly beyond that of the more traditional collections. This surely will give no offence to ears familiar with such things as Bartok's "Music for Children" or Britten's folk-song arrangements which have, I suppose, been my unconscious models in some instances.

My grateful thanks are due to everyone who has helped and advised me, but especially to Donald Mitchell, without whose initial friendly encouragement the task would never have been undertaken.

ERIC ROSEBERRY

CONTENTS

1. LOOK, A STAR SHINES

A traditional Polish carol, *Świeci Gwiazda Jezusowi.*

2. I SAW THREE SHIPS COME SAILING BY

Gently flowing

VOICES

PIANO

p

with pedal

1. I saw three ships come sail - ing by,

Sail - ing by, (echo) sail - ing by, I saw three ships come sail - ing by, On

Christ - mas Day in the morn - ing.

sf

CODA

1 I saw three ships come sailing by,
   Sailing by, sailing by,
 I saw three ships come sailing by,
   On Christmas Day in the morning.

2 And what do you think was in them then,
   In them then, in them then,
 And what do you think was in them then,
   On Christmas Day in the morning?

3 Three pretty girls were in them then,
   In them then, in them then,
 Three pretty girls were in them then,
   On Christmas Day in the morning.

4 And one could whistle and one could sing,
   The other play on the violin.
 Such joy there was at my wedding
   On Christmas Day in the morning.

An old English Nursery Rhyme.

3. I SAW THREE SHIPS COME SAILING IN

★Play the grace-note in v. 1 only.

1 I saw three ships come sailing in,
    On Christmas Day, on Christmas Day,
I saw three ships come sailing in,
    On Christmas Day in the morning.

2 And what was in those ships all three?

3 Our Saviour Christ and his lady.

4 Pray, whither sailed those ships all three?

5 O, they sailed into Bethlehem.

6 And all the bells on earth shall ring,

7 And all the angels in heaven shall sing,

8 And all the souls on earth shall sing.

9 Then let us all rejoice amain!

From Sandys' *Christmas Carols,* 1833.

4. GOD REST YOU MERRY, GENTLEMEN

(omit this bar in v. 8)

CODA

1 God rest you merry, gentlemen,
   Let nothing you dismay,
Remember Christ our Saviour
   Was born on Christmas Day,
To save poor souls from Satan's power
   That had long time gone astray,
O tidings of comfort and joy.

2 From God that is our Father,
   The blessèd angels came,
Unto some certain shepherds,
   With tidings of the same;
That there was born in Bethlehem,
   The Son of God by name.
O tidings, etc.

3 Go, fear not, said God's angels,
   Let nothing you affright,
For there is born in Bethlehem,
   Of a pure Virgin bright,
One able to advance you,
   And threw down Satan quite.
O tidings, etc.

4 The shepherds at those tidings,
   Rejoiced much in mind,
And left their flocks a-feeding
   In tempest storms of wind,
And strait they came to Bethlehem,
   The Son of God to find.
O tidings, etc.

5 Now when they came to Bethlehem,
   Where our sweet Saviour lay,
They found Him in a manger,
   Where oxen feed on hay,
The blessèd Virgin kneeling down,
   Unto the Lord did pray.
O tidings, etc.

6 With sudden joy and gladness,
   The shepherds were beguil'd,
To see the Babe of Israel,
   Before his mother mild,
On them with joy and cheerfulness,
   Rejoice each mother's child.
O tidings, etc.

7 Now to the Lord sing praises,
   All you within this place,
Like we true loving brethren,
   Each other to embrace,
For the merry time of Christmas,
   Is drawing on apace.
O tidings, etc.

8 God bless the ruler of this house,
   And send him long to reign,
And many a merry Christmas
   May live to see again.
Among your friends and kindred,
   That live both far and near,
And God send you a happy New Year.

Words from Sandys' *Christmas Carols*, 1833 (West of England).
Tune from a London broadsheet of about 1800.

5. THE FIRST NOWELL

★The notes in brackets may be omitted.

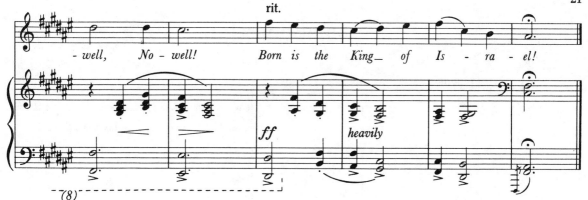

- well, No - well! Born is the King of Is - ra - el!

rit.

ff

heavily

(8)

1 The first Nowell the angel did say
Was to certain poor shepherds in fields
as they lay;
In fields where they lay, keeping their
sheep,
In a cold winter's night that was so
deep:
Nowell, Nowell, Nowell, Nowell,
Born is the King of Israel!

2 They looked up and saw a star,
Shining in the east, beyond them far;
And to the earth it gave great light,
And so it continued both day and night:
Nowell, etc.

3 And by the light of that same star,
Three Wise Men came from country
far;
To seek for a King was their intent,
And to follow the star wheresoever it
went:
Nowell, etc.

4 This star drew nigh to the north-west;
O'er Bethlehem it took its rest,
And there it did both stop and stay
Right over the place where Jesus lay:
Nowell, etc.

5 Then did they know assurèdly
Within that house the King did lie:
One entered in then for to see,
And found the Babe in poverty:
Nowell, etc.

6 Then entered in those Wise Men three,
Fell reverently upon their knee,
And offered there in His presence
Both gold and myrrh and frankincense:
Nowell, etc.

7 Between an ox-stall and an ass
This Child truly there born He was;
For want of clothing they did Him lay
All in the manger, among the hay:
Nowell, etc.

8 Then let us all with one accord
Sing praises to our heavenly Lord,
That hath made heaven and earth of
naught,
And with His blood mankind hath
bought:
Nowell, etc.

9 If we in our time shall do well,
We shall be free from death and hell;
For God hath prepared for us all
A resting place in general:
Nowell, etc.

From Sandys' *Christmas Carols,* 1833.

6. GOOD KING WENCESLAS

gath-'ring win-ter fu - el.

1 Good King Wenceslas looked out,
  On the Feast of Stephen,
When the snow lay round about,
  Deep, and crisp, and even:
Brightly shone the moon that night,
  Though the frost was cruel,
When a poor man came in sight,
  Gathering winter fuel.

2 "Hither, page, and stand by me,
  If thou know'st it, telling,
Yonder peasant, who is he?
  Where and what his dwelling?"
"Sire, he lives a good league hence,
  Underneath the mountain,
Right against the forest fence,
  By Saint Agnes' fountain."

3 "Bring me flesh, and bring me wine,
  Bring me pine-logs hither:
Thou and I will see him dine,
  When we bear them thither."
Page and monarch, forth they went,
  Forth they went together;
Through the rude wind's wild lament
  And the bitter weather.

4 "Sire, the night is darker now,
  And the wind blows stronger;
Fails my heart, I know not how;
  I can go no longer."
"Mark my footsteps, good my page;
  Tread thou in them boldly:
Thou shalt find the winter's rage
  Freeze thy blood less coldly."

5 In his master's steps he trod,
  Where the snow lay dinted;
Heat was in the very sod
  Which the Saint had printed.
Therefore, Christian men, be sure,
  Wealth or rank possessing,
Ye who now will bless the poor,
  Shall yourselves find blessing.

Words by J. M. Neale (1833) substituted for the Spring Carol,
Tempus adest floridum. Melody from *Piae Cantiones*, 1582.

7. CRADLE SONG

Gently moving

VOICES

PIANO

p very smoothly

1. Jo - seph dear - est, Jo - seph mine, Help me cra - dle the child di - vine;
2. Glad - ly, dear one, la - dy mine, Help I cra - dle this child of thine;

God reward thee and all that's thine In Pa - ra - dise, So prays the mo - ther
God's own light on us both shall shine In Pa - ra - dise, As prays the mo - ther

1. Ma - ry.
2. Ma - ry. *He came a-mong us at Christ-mas tide, At Christ-mas tide, In*

Beth - le - hem; Men shall bring Him from far and wide Love's di - a - dem:

Je - sus, Je - sus, Lo, He comes, and loves, and saves, and frees us!

CODA

p very smoothly

1 Joseph dearest, Joseph mine,
  Help me cradle the Child divine;
  God reward thee and all that's thine
    In Paradise,
      So prays the mother Mary.

2 Gladly, dear one, lady mine,
  Help I cradle this Child of thine;
  God's own light on us both shall shine
    In Paradise,
      As prays the mother Mary.

He came among us at Christmas tide,
  At Christmas tide,
    In Bethlehem;
Men shall bring Him from far and wide
    Love's diadem:
    Jesus, Jesus,
Lo, He comes, and loves, and saves,
  and frees us!

3 *Servant* (1)
  Peace to all that have goodwill!
  God, who heaven and earth doth fill,
  Comes to turn us away from ill,
    And lies so still
      Within the crib of Mary.

4 *Servant* (2)
  All shall come and bow the knee:
  Wise and happy their souls shall be,
  Loving such a divinity,
    As all may see
      In Jesus, Son of Mary.
  He came among us at Christmas tide, etc.

5 *Servant* (3)
Now is born Emmanuel,
Prophesied once by Ezekiel,
Promised Mary by Gabriel—
   Ah, who can tell
      Thy praises, Son of Mary!

6 *Servant* (4)
Thou my lazy heart hast stirred,
Thou, the Father's eternal Word,
Greater than aught that ear hath heard,
   Thou tiny bird
      Of love, thou Son of Mary.
He came among us at Christmas tide, etc.

7 *Servant* (1)
Sweet and lovely little one,
Thou princely, beautiful, God's own
   Son,
Without Thee all of us were undone;
   Our love is won
      By Thine, O Son of Mary.

8 *Servant* (2)
Little man, and God indeed,
Little and poor, Thou art all we need;
We will follow where Thou dost lead,
   And we will heed
      Our brother, born of Mary.
He came among us at Christmas tide, etc.

The words occur in a Leipzig University MS.,
c.1500, as part of a mystery play acted in
church around the crib. Translated by Percy
Dearmer.

8. WE WISH YOU A MERRY CHRISTMAS

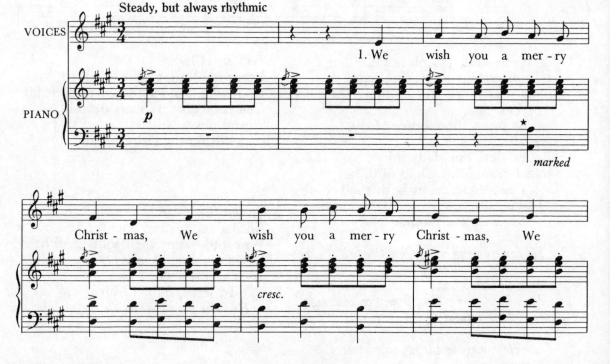

★The octaves are optional; if preferred, the lower note only may be played.

wish you a mer-ry Christ-mas, And a Hap-py New Year! Good.

tid-ings we bring To you and your kin, We

wish you a mer-ry Christ-mas And a hap-py New Year!

★The notes in brackets may be omitted.

1 We wish you a Merry Christmas,
We wish you a Merry Christmas,
We wish you a Merry Christmas
And a Happy New Year!
Good tidings, etc.

2 Now bring us some figgy pudding,
Now bring us some figgy pudding,
Now bring us some figgy pudding,
Now bring some to us here.
Good tidings, etc.

3 We won't go until we get it,
We won't go until we get it,
We won't go until we get it,
So bring some right here.
Good tidings, etc.

4 We all like our figgy pudding,
We all like our figgy pudding,
So bring us some figgy pudding,
With all its good cheer!
Good tidings, etc.

A traditional English carol.

9. ROCKING

1 Little Jesus, sweetly sleep, do not stir;
We will lend a coat of fur,
    We will rock you, rock you, rock you,
    We will rock you, rock you, rock you:
See the fur to keep you warm,
Snugly round your tiny form.

2 Mary's little baby, sleep, sweetly sleep,
Sleep in comfort, slumber deep;
    We will rock you, rock you, rock you,
    We will rock you, rock you, rock you,
We will serve you all we can,
Darling, darling little man.

A Czech carol *Hajej, nynjej*, collected by Miss Jacubickova and translated by Percy Dearmer.

10. THE SEVEN JOYS OF MARY

Fast and bouyantly

1. The first good joy that Ma - ry had, It was the joy of one;_____ To see the bless - èd Je - sus Christ When He was first her Son:_____ *When He was first her Son, good Man:_* And *bless - ed may He be,_____ Both Fa - ther, Son and Ho - ly Ghost, To*

CODA

senza rit.

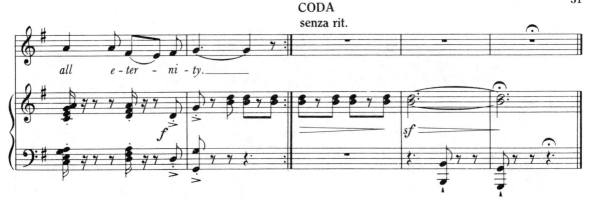

all e - ter - ni - ty.

1 The first good joy that Mary had,
    It was the joy of one;
  To see the blessèd Jesus Christ
    When He was first her Son:

  When He was first her Son, good Man:
    And blessed may He be,
  Both Father, Son, and Holy Ghost,
    To all eternity.

2 The next good joy that Mary had,
    It was the joy of two;
  To see her own son, Jesus Christ
    Making the lame to go:
  When He was first, etc.

3 The next good joy that Mary had,
    It was the joy of three;
  To see her own son, Jesus Christ
    Making the blind to see:
  When He was first, etc.

4 The next good joy that Mary had,
    It was the joy of four;
  To see her own son, Jesus Christ
    Reading the Bible o'er:
  When He was first, etc.

5 The next good joy that Mary had,
    It was the joy of five;
  To see her own son, Jesus Christ
    Raising the dead to life:
  When He was first, etc.

6 The next good joy that Mary had,
    It was the joy of six;
  To see her own son, Jesus Christ
    Rise from the crucifix:
  When He was first, etc.

7 The next good joy that Mary had,
    It was the joy of seven;
  To see her own son, Jesus Christ
    Ascending into heaven:
  When He was first, etc.

A traditional English carol.

11. WHAT IS THIS FRAGRANCE?

(Quelle est cette odeur agréable?)

Peacefully flowing

VOICES

PIANO

pp *p*

with pedal

1. What is this fra - grance soft - ly steal - ing?

Shep-herds! It sets my heart a - stir! Ne -ver was sweet - ness

(like flutes)

so ap - peal - ing— Ne -ver were flowers of spring so fair!

more warmly

What is this fra - grance soft - ly steal - ing? Shep-herds! It

sets   my   heart   a – stir!

1 What is this fragrance softly stealing?
Shepherds! It sets my heart astir!
Never was sweetness so appealing—
Never were flowers of spring so fair!
What is this fragrance softly stealing?
Shepherds! It sets my heart astir!

2 What is this light around us streaming?
Out of the dark—with blinding ray—
Purer than Star of Morning's seeming—
Showing our path as plain as day!
What is this light around us streaming?
Out of the dark—with blinding ray!

3 What is this wonder all around us
Filling the air with music light!
Shepherds! Some magic here hath found us!
Never mine ears knew such delight!
What is this wonder all around us
Filling the air with music light!

4 Be not affrighted, shepherds lowly!
Harken the Angel of the Lord!
Bearing a message glad and holy—
Shedding a radiance all abroad!
Be not affrighted, shepherds lowly!
Harken the Angel of the Lord!

5 There, in a manger with His mother,
Lieth our Saviour, born today!
Come away shepherds; let none other
Hinder thy coming now away!
There, in a manger with His mother,
Lieth our Saviour, born today!

6 God in His charity and favour,
Give of His grace to all a share!
Grace that aboundeth, now and ever,
Peace that abideth everywhere!
God in His charity and favour,
Give of His grace to all a share!

A French Noël, *Quelle est cette odeur agréable?* (Lorraine), translated by K. W. Simpson.

12. THE HOLLY AND THE IVY

CODA

sing - ing in the choir.

p

1 The holly and the ivy,
   When they are both full grown,
   Of all the trees that are in the wood,
   The holly bears the crown:

   The rising of the sun
   And the running of the deer,
   The playing of the merry organ,
   Sweet singing in the choir.

2 The holly bears a blossom,
   As white as the lily flower,
   And Mary bore sweet Jesus Christ,
   To be our sweet Saviour:
   The rising, etc.

3 The holly bears a berry,
   As red as any blood,
   And Mary bore sweet Jesus Christ
   To do poor sinners good:
   The rising, etc.

4 The holly bears a prickle,
   As sharp as any thorn,
   And Mary bore sweet Jesus Christ
   On Christmas day in the morn:
   The rising, etc.

5 The holly bears a bark,
   As bitter as any gall,
   And Mary bore sweet Jesus Christ
   For to redeem us all:
   The rising, etc.

6 The holly and the ivy,
   When they are both full grown,
   Of all the trees that are in the wood,
   The holly bears the crown.
   The rising, etc.

Words and melody taken from Mrs. Clayton at Chipping Campden,
Glos. (supplemented by words from Mrs. Wyatt, East Harptree,
Somerset) by Cecil J. Sharp.

13. INFANT HOLY, INFANT LOWLY

1. In-fant ho - ly, In-fant low - ly, For His bed a cat - tle stall,

Ox - en low - ing lit - tle know - ing Christ the Babe is

Lord of all. Swifts are wing - ing, an-gels sing - ing, No-ëls ring - ing,

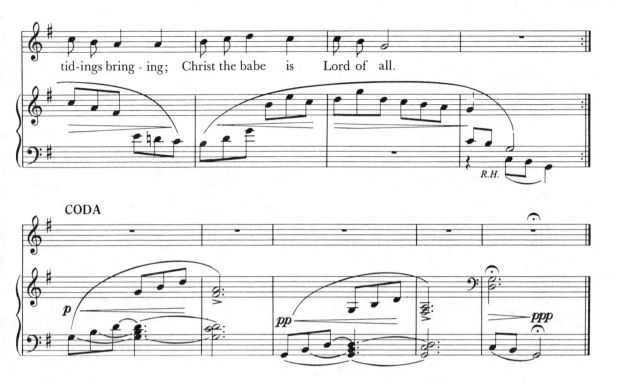

tid-ings bring - ing; Christ the babe is Lord of all.

R.H.

CODA

1 Infant holy, Infant lowly,
   For His bed a cattle stall,
   Oxen lowing little knowing
   Christ the Babe is Lord of all.
   Swifts are winging, angels singing,
   Noëls ringing, tidings bringing;
   Christ the Babe is Lord of all.

2 Flocks were sleeping, shepherds keeping
   Vigil 'till the morning new.
   Saw the glory, heard the story,
   Tidings of a gospel true.
   Thus rejoicing, free from sorrow,
   Praises voicing greet the morrow,
   Christ the Babe is born for you.

An old Polish carol, *W żłobie leży*, translated by E. M. G. Reed.

14. A VIRGIN MOST PURE

-gres - sion hath wrapped___ us in: Aye and there - fore _ be_ mer - ry, re - joice and be you mer - ry, Set sor - rows_ a - -side; Christ Je - sus_ our_ Sa - viour was born on this tide.

f slightly detached

ff

8va bassa - - - - - - - - - - - - - - - - - -

CODA

p

14. A VIRGIN MOST PURE

(Alternative Version)

★F♯ may be used here as a variant.

(v. 7)

- side; Christ Je - sus— our— Sa - viour was born on this tide. tide.

1 A Virgin most pure, as the prophets do tell,
Hath brought forth a baby, as it hath befel,
To be our Redeemer from death, hell, and sin,
Which Adam's transgression hath wrapped us in:
Aye and therefore be merry, rejoice and be you merry,
Set sorrows aside;
Christ Jesus our Saviour was born on this tide.

2 At Bethl'em in Jewry a city there was,
Where Joseph and Mary together did pass,
And there to be taxed with many one mo',
For Caesar commanded the same should be so:
Aye and therefore, etc.

3 But when they had entered the city so fair,
A number of people so mighty was there,
That Joseph and Mary, whose substance was small,
Could find in the inn there no lodging at all:
Aye and therefore, etc.

From Davies Gilbert, *Some Ancient Christmas Carols*, 1822. Traditional words and melody (in the 7th mode).

4 Then were they constrained in a stable to lie,
Where horses and asses they used for to tie;
Their lodging so simple they took it no scorn;
But against the next morning our Saviour was born:
Aye and therefore, etc.

5 The King of all Kings to this world being brought,
Small store of fine linen to wrap Him was sought;
And when she had swaddled her young Son so sweet,
Within an ox-manger she laid Him to sleep:
Aye and therefore, etc.

6 Then God sent an angel from heaven so high,
To certain poor shepherds in fields where they lie,
And bade them no longer in sorrow to stay,
Because that our Saviour was born on this day:
Aye and therefore, etc.

7 Then presently after the shepherds did spy
A number of angels that stood in the sky;
They joyfully talked, and sweetly did sing,
To God be all glory, our heavenly King:
Aye and therefore, etc.

15. GREENSLEEVES

Seriously, but with movement

VOICES

PIANO

1. The old year now away is fled, The new year it is

en-ter-èd; Then let us now our sins down-tread, And joy-ful-ly all ap-

-pear: Let's mer-ry be this day, And let us now both

sport and play: Hang grief, cast care a-way! God send you a hap-py New

Year._____   2. The

1 The old year now away is fled,
    The new year it is enterèd;
His hands and feet were wounded deep,

1 The old year now away is fled,
    The new year it is enterèd;
 Then let us now our sins down-tread,
    And joyfully all appear:
      Let's merry be this day,
      And let us now both sport and play:
      Hang grief, cast care away!
      God send you a happy New Year!

2 The name-day now of Christ we keep,
    Who for our sins did often weep;
 His hands and feet were wounded deep,
    And His blessèd side with a spear;
      His head they crowned with thorn,
      And at Him they did laugh and scorn,
      Who for our good was born:
      God send us a happy New Year!

3 And now with New Year's gifts each friend
    Unto each other they do send:
 God grant we may all our lives amend,
    And that the truth may appear.
      Now, like the snake, your skin
      Cast off, of evil thoughts and sin,
      And so the year begin:
      God send us a happy New Year!

A Waits' carol from *New Christmas Carols*, 1642 ('to the tune of
Greensleeves'), in the unique black-letter collection of Antony à Wood,
now in the Bodleian.

16. OUR BLESSÈD LADY'S LULLABY

Keyboard part taken
from William Byrd

1. Up-on my lap_ my Sov-'reign sits,_ And feeds up-on_ my breast;_ Mean-while, His love_ sus-tains my life_ And gives my bo - dy rest.____ When Thou hast ta - ken Thy re-past, Re-pose_ my Babe_ on me;___ So may_ Thy mo - ther and__ Thy nurse, Thy cra - dle al - so_ be.____ Sing_

lul - la-by my lit - tle Boy, My life's joy lul - la - by.

1 Upon my lap my Sovereign sits,
   And feeds upon my breast;
   Meanwhile, His love sustains my life
   And gives my body rest.
       When Thou hast taken Thy repast,
       Repose my Babe on me;
       So may Thy mother and Thy nurse,
       Thy cradle also be.
           Sing lullaby my little Boy,
           My life's joy lullaby.

2 The earth is now a heaven become,
   And this base power of mine
   A princely palace unto me,
   My Son doth make to shine.
       This sight I see, this Child I have,
       This Infant I embrace,
       O endless Comfort of the earth
       And heaven's eternal Grace.
           Sing lullaby, etc.

3 My Babe, my Bliss, my Child, my Choice,
   My Fruit, my Flower and Bud,
   My Jesus and my only Joy,
   The sum of all my good.
       Three Kings their treasures hither brought,
       Of incense, myrrh and gold,
       The heavens' treasure and the King
       That here they might behold.
           Sing lullaby, etc.

4 And let th'ensuing blessèd race
   Thou wilt succeeding raise,
   Join all their praises unto mine,
   To multiply their praise.
       And let th'ensuing blessèd race
       Thou wilt succeeding raise,
       Join all their praises unto mine,
       To multiply their praise.
           Sing lullaby, etc.

Tune, *Sellenger's Round* (16th century), set to
words by Richard Rowlands alias Verstegen.

17. HE IS BORN
(Il est né)

He is born, the Holy One!
Let thy joyful music ring!
He is born, the Holy One!
Greet with song the new-born King!

1

Full four thousand years ago
   Prophets told that He should be!
Full four thousand years ago
   Sang they of His majesty!
He is born, etc.

2

In a manger He did lie,
   Cradled in humility!
In a manger He did lie,
   On a gentle maiden's knee.
He is born, etc.

★Always **pp**

VERSES ★

3

O how beautiful is He!
  Perfected in heavenly grace!
O how beautiful is He!
  Joyfully behold His face!
He is born, etc.

4

For thy love He seeks alway!
  He was born thy heart to find!
For thy love He seeks alway!
  Turn to Him in spirit kind!
He is born, etc.

5

Greet Him, Princes of the East!
  Come, the Infant to adore!
Greet Him, Princes of the East!
  Loud your happy praises pour!
He is born, etc.

6

Herod sought Him near and far!
  And His tender mother fled!
Herod sought Him near and far!
  But the Babe was sheltered.
He is born, etc.

7

Satan held us in his thrall!
  Loud he mocked us in his pride!
Satan held us in his thrall!
  Till for us the Saviour died!
He is born, etc.

8

All our bitter debts He paid!
  Lift your hearts and thankful be!
All our bitter debts He paid!
  Praise Him then eternally!
He is born, etc.

★Dynamics should be varied to suit the expression of the words.

Melody and words from *Dictionnaire de Noëls*. English translation by K. W. Simpson.

18. THERE IS NO ROSE

Freely and with feeling

ALTO

1. There is no rose of____ such____ vir - tue
3. By that____ rose we____ may____ well_ see
5. Leave we____ all this____ world - ly__ mirth,

TENOR (DIV.)

PIANO (for rehearsal only)

Freely and with feeling

As is the rose____ as__ bare____ Je - su.
That he is God____ in__ per - sons_ three,
And fol - low we____ this_ joy - ful__ birth;

(UNIS.)

Al - le - lu - ia.
Pa - ri - for - ma.
Tran - se - a - mus.

A mediæval carol.

19. NOVA, NOVA

Nova, nova; Ave fit ex Eva.
1 Gabriel of high degree,
He came down from Trinity,
From Nazareth to Galilee:
   Nova, nova.

Nova, nova; Ave fit ex Eva.
2 I met a maiden in a place;
I kneeled down afore her face
And said: Hail, Mary, full of grace;
   Nova, nova.

Nova, nova; Ave fit ex Eva.
3 When the maiden heard tell of this,
She was full sore abashed y-wis,
And weened that she had done amiss;
   Nova, nova.

Nova, nova; Ave fit ex Eva.
4 Then said the angel: Dread not thou,
For ye be conceived with great virtue
Whose name shall be called Jesu;
   Nova, nova.

Nova, nova; Ave fit ex Eva.
5 It is not yet six weeks agone
Sin Elizabeth conceived John
As it was prophesied beforn;
   Nova, nova.

Nova, nova; Ave fit ex Eva.
6 Then said the maiden: Verily,
I am your servant right truly;
Ecce, ancilla Domini;
   Nova, nova.

Nova, nova; Ave fit ex Eva.

From a 15th century Glasgow manuscript.

20. THE SHEPHERDS WENT THEIR HASTY WAY

Light and flowing

1. The shep-herds went their has - ty way, And found the low - ly

sta - ble shed Where the Vir - gin Mo - ther lay;

Now they check'd their ea - ger tread, For to__ the Babe__ that

to__ her clung, A mo - ther's song__ the Vir - gin sung.

★ In this arrangement, the Altos, Tenors and Basses should hum while the Sopranos sing the words.

1 The shepherds went their hasty way,
   And found the lowly stable shed
Where the Virgin Mother lay;
   Now they checked their eager tread,
For to the Babe that to her clung,
   A mother's song the Virgin sung.

2 They told her how a glorious light,
   Far streaming from a heavenly throng,
Round them shone suspending night!
   While more sweet than mother's song
Blest angels hailed the Saviour's birth;
   Glory to God, and peace on earth.

3 She listened to the tale divine,
   And closer still the Babe she prest;
While she cried, the Babe is mine,
   Mother-love o'er flowed her breast:
Joy rose within her like summer's morn:
   Peace, peace on earth; its Prince is born.

4 Then (cried she) is my soul elate,
   That strife should vanish, battle cease;
Poor am I, of low estate,
   Mother of the Prince of Peace.
Joy rises in me like a summer's morn;
   Peace, peace on earth; its Prince is born.

Words, a cento from S. T. Coleridge. Melody an old Alsatian carol.

21. THE BABE IN BETHL'EM'S MANGER

birth: All hail His com-ing down to earth, Who rais-es us to heaven..

1 The Babe in Bethl'em's manger laid,
　In humble form so low,
By wond'ring angels is survey'd,
　Thro' all His scenes of woe.
　　Nowell, Nowell O sing a Saviour's birth:
　　All hail His coming down to earth,
　　Who raises us to heaven.

2 For not to sit on David's throne
　With worldly pomp and joy,
He came for sinners to atone,
　And Satan to destroy.
　　Nowell, etc.

3 To preach the word of life divine,
　To give the living bread,
To heal the sick with hand benign,
　And raise to life the dead.
　　Nowell, etc.

4 Well may we sing the Saviour's birth
　Who need the grace so given,
And hail His coming down to earth,
　Who raises us to heaven.
　　Nowell, etc.

An old Kentish carol. Words and melody traditional.

22. HAIL, MARY, FULL OF GRACE

Hail, Ma-ry, full of grace, Mo-ther in ___

Hail, Ma-ry, full of grace, Mo-ther in ___

Hail, Ma-ry, full of grace, Mo-ther in ___

vir - gi - ni - ty. ___

vir - gi - ni - ty. ___

vir - gi-ni - ty. ___

VERSES
SOPRANO

1. The Ho - ly Ghost is to thee sent From the
2. ⁊ When the an - gel *A* - *ve* be - gan, Flesh_ and
3. So saith the gos - pel of Saint John: God_ and
4. ⁊ And the pro - phet Je - re - my Told in his
5. ⁊ Much - ë joy to us was grant And_ in
6. ⁊ Ma - ry, grant_ us the bliss, There_ thy

TENOR

Fa - ther om - ni - po - tent; Now is God with-
blood___ to - ge - ther___ ran; Ma - ry bore both
man___ is_ made but___ one, In flesh and blood, bo-
pro - - - phe - cy That the Son of
ear - thë_ peace y - plant, When that born was
Son - nës_ won - ing___ is; Of that we han

-in thee went, When the an - gel said *A* - *ve*.
God and man Through vir - tue and through_ dig - ni - ty.
-dy and bone, One God in per - son - ës___ three.
Ma - - ry Should die for us_ on rood - ë___ tree.
this _ 'fant In the land_ of Ga - li - lee.
done a - miss Pray for us___ *pour cha - ri - té*.

A mediæval carol.

23. QUEM PASTORES

1 Quem pastores laudavere,
  Quibus angeli dixere,
  Absit vobis jam timere,
    Natus est rex gloriæ.

2 Ad quem magi ambulabant,
  Aurum, thus, myrrham portabant,
  Immolabant hæc sincere
    Nato regi gloriæ.

3 Christo regi, Deo nato,
  Per Mariam nobis dato,
  Merito resonet vere
    Laus, honor et gloria.

This carol occurs in V. Triller, 1555, *Leisentritt*, 1567, Schein's
Cantionale, 1627, and elsewhere.

24. BETHLEHEM

Arranged by
Charles Gounod
(1818 — 1893)

Gently rocking

SOPRANO
ALTO

TENOR
BASS

1. In that poor sta - ble How charm - ing Je - sus lies, Words are not

a - ble To fa - thom His em - prise! _____ No pa - lace of a

King _____ Can show so rare a thing _____ In his - to - ry or

fa - ble As that of which we sing In that poor sta - ble.

1   In that poor stable
How charming Jesus lies,
    Words are not able
To fathom His emprise!
No palace of a King
Can show so rare a thing
In history or fable
As that of which we sing
    In that poor stable.

2   See here God's power
In weakness fortifies
    This infant hour
Of Love's epiphanies!
Our foe is now despoiled,
The wiles of hell are foiled;
On earth there grows a flower
Pure, undefiled, unsoiled—
    See here God's power!

3   Though far from knowing
The Babe's Divinity,
    Mine eyes are growing
To see His majesty;
For lo! the new-born Child
Upon me sweetly smiled,
The gift of faith bestowing;
Thus I my Lord descry,
    Though far from knowing.

4   No more affliction!
For God endures our pains;
    In crucifixion
The Son victorious reigns.
For us the sufferer brings
Salvation in His wings;
To win our souls' affection
Could He, the King of Kings,
    Know more affliction?

1   Dans cette étable
Que Jésus est charmant,
    Qu'il est aimable
Dans cet abaissement!
Que d'attraits à la fois!
Tous les palais des rois
N'ont rien de comparable
Aux charmes que je vois
    Dans cette étable!

2   Que sa puissance
Paraît bien en ce jour,
    Malgré l'enfance
Où l'a réduit l'amour!
Notre ennemi dompté,
L'enfer deconcerté,
Font voir qu'en sa naissance
Rien n'est si redouté
    Que sa puissance.

3   Sans le connaître,
Dans sa divinité
    Je vois paraître
Toute sa majesté;
Dans cet enfant qui naît,
A son aspect qui plait,
Je découvre mon maître
Et je sens ce qu'il est
    Sans le connaître.

4   Plus de misère!
Un Dieu souffre pour nous
    Et de son père
Apaise le courroux;
C'est en notre favour
Qu'il naît dans la douleur;
Pouvait-il pour nous plaire
Unir à sa grandeur
    Plus de misère?

A traditional French carol. Words by Fléchier,
translated by Maurice F. Bell.

25. HERE WE COME A-WASSAILING

With a swing

VOICES

1. Here we come a-was-sail-ing A-mong the leaves so green,___ Here we come a-wan-der-ing, So fair__ to be seen: *Love and joy come to you,* *And to you your was-sail* too, *And God bless you, and send__ you a hap-py New*

PIANO

Year,   And God   send   you   a   hap - py New Year.

1 Here we come a-wassailing
   Among the leaves so green,
Here we come a-wandering,
   So fair to be seen:
      Love and joy come to you,
      And to you your wassail too,
      And God bless you, and send you
      A happy New Year.

2 Our wassail cup is made
   Of the rosemary tree;
And so is your beer
   Of the best barley:
      Love and joy, etc.

3 We are not daily beggars
   That beg from door to door,
But we are neighbours' children
   Whom you have seen before:
      Love and joy, etc.

4 Call up the butler of this house,
   Put on his golden ring;
Let him bring us up a glass of beer,
   And better we shall sing:
      Love and joy, etc.

5 We have got a little purse
   Of stretching leather skin;
We want a little of your money
   To line it well within:
      Love and joy, etc.

6 Bring us out a table,
   And spread it with a cloth;
Bring us out a mouldy cheese,
   And some of your Christmas loaf:
      Love and joy, etc.

7 God bless the master of this house,
   Likewise the mistress too;
And all the little children
   That round the table go:
      Love and joy, etc.

8 Good Master and good Mistress,
   While you're sitting by the fire,
Pray think of us poor children
   Who are wandering in the mire:
      Love and joy, etc.

Words from Husk's *Songs of the Nativity*, 1808.

64

26. CHRISIMAS DAY

1 There was a pig went out to dig,
  Chrisimas day, Chrisimas day,
There was a pig went out to dig
  On Chrisimas day in the morning.

2 There was a cow went out to plough.

3 There was a sparrow went out to harrow.

4 There was a drake went out to rake.

5 There was a crow went out to sow.

6 There was a sheep went out to reap.

A traditional Lancashire carol.

66

27. JESUS CHRIST IS BORN TONIGHT

1 Jesus Christ is born tonight, how happy we will be.
  All the angels sing in heaven merrily as we:
  Gloria, gloria in excelsis Deo,
  Gloria, gloria in excelsis Deo!

2 In the stable ox and donkey humbly kneel and pray,
  Since they know that God, the Saviour, has been born
      today.
  Gloria, gloria in excelsis Deo,
  Gloria, gloria in excelsis Deo!

A traditional Polish carol, *Narodził się Jezus Chrystus.*

28. AS JOSEPH WAS A-WALKING

As Jo - seph was a - walk - ing, he
heard an an - gel sing:_____ "This night there shall be born_____ on

★The inner notes may be omitted.

earth_ our heaven - ly King._____   *very smoothly*

He nei - ther shall be cloth - èd in

pur - ple or in pall,_____ But_ in the fair_ white lin - en that

us - en ba - bies all._____

rit.   **a little slower**
peaceful

He nei - ther shall be

70

Traditional English words set
to a traditional French melody.

29. THE ANGEL GABRIEL

1 The angel Gabriel from heaven came,
His wings as drifted snow, his eyes as flame,
"All hail," said he, "thou lowly maiden Mary,
   Most highly favoured lady,"
      Gloria!

2 "For known a blessèd mother thou shalt be,
All generations laud and honour thee,
Thy Son shall be Emmanuel, by seers foretold.
   Most highly favoured lady,"
      Gloria!

3 Then gentle Mary meekly bowed her head,
"To me be as it pleaseth God," she said,
"My soul shall laud and magnify His Holy Name."
   Most highly favoured lady,
      Gloria!

4 Of her, Emmanuel, the Christ, was born
In Bethlehem, all on a Christmas morn,
And Christian folk throughout the world will ever
   say—
   Most highly favoured lady,
      Gloria!

Melody collected by Father Donostia. Words by S. Baring Gould.

30. UNTO US A BOY IS BORN

(Puer nobis)

sleep-y cows and ass – es; But the ve-ry beasts could see That

He all men sur-pass – – – – – – es.

TENORS AND BASSES

3. He-rod then with fear was filled: "A

f

without pedal

brutal

prince," he said, "in Jew – ry!" All the lit-tle boys he killed At

Beth-l'em in his fu - - - - - - ry.

SOPRANOS AND ALTOS

4. Now may Ma - ry's Son, who came So long a - go to

TENORS AND BASSES

5. O - me - ga and Al - pha

love us, Lead us all with hearts a - flame Un - to the joys a -

He! Let the or - gan thun - - -

The words and original melody of *Puer nobis nascitur* are in a Trier MS. of the 15th century.
The melody in this form is in *Piae Cantiones*, 1582. Words translated by Percy Dearmer.

31. NOËL! A NEW NOËL!
(Noël nouvelet)

Gently flowing

VOICES

1. No - ël! A new No - ël! Here to - ge - ther

PIANO

p

with pedal

sing! Faith - ful peo - ple cry - ing "Lord, our thanks we

bring," Sing - ing a No - ël for the Sa - viour King.

Sing a new No - ël, Let your glad voi - ces ring.

1 Noël! A new Noël!
Here together sing!
Faithful people crying
"Lord, our thanks we bring,"
Singing a Noël for the Saviour King.
Sing a new Noël,
Let your glad voices ring.

2 Clearly spake the Angel:
"Shepherds, come away!
Peaceful and rejoicing
Bethl'em seek this day!
A little Lamb is born to be our King!"
Sing a new Noël,
Let your glad voices ring.

3 There they found together
Joseph—Mary blest—
Cradling 'gainst the weather
Jesus at her breast.
Only a manger for the heavenly King!
Sing a new Noël,
Let your glad voices ring.

4 Kings draw nigh to greet Him,
Neath the burning star,
Seeking Bethl'em city
From their countries far.
Here, in the dawning light, they find their King.
Sing a new Noël,
Let your glad voices ring.

5 See! one beareth incense,
Others, gold and myrrh!
Offering them to Jesus
Sleeping sweetly there.
See! the poor manger is a-blossoming!
Sing a new Noël,
Let your glad voices ring.

6 See our Jesu Saviour
Who, by His great deeds
From despair will save us,
Dying for our needs.
Shedding His blood, that all the world may sing,
Sing a new Noël,
Let your glad voices ring.

A Provençal carol, *Noël nouvelet*, translated by K. W. Simpson.

32. SUO-GÂN

1 Suo-gân, do not weep,
  Suo-gân, go to sleep,
  Suo-gân, mother's near,
  Suo-gân, have no fear.

2 Suo-gân, eastern star,
  Suo-gân, from afar,
  Suo-gân, shepherds sing,
  Suo-gân, new-born King.

3 Suo-gân, from above,
  Suo-gân, song of love,
  Suo-gân, blessèd morn,
  Suo-gân, Christ is born.

A Welsh melody. English words by Frank Foster.

82

33. HARK TO THE ANGELS

Version I: Male voices

Version II: S.A.T.B.

lightly — Born on this day in Beth-le-hem town is Christ the Lord, Christ the Lord.

Born on this day in Beth-le-hem town is Christ the _ Lord, Christ the Lord.

Born on this day in Beth-le-hem town is Christ the Lord, Christ the Lord.

Born on this day in Beth-le-hem town is Christ the Lord, Christ the Lord.

lightly · sustained

Version III: Voices and Piano

Vigorously

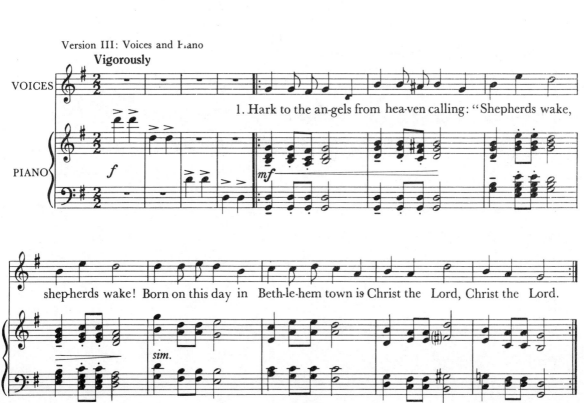

VOICES

1. Hark to the an-gels from hea-ven calling: "Shepherds wake,

PIANO

shep-herds wake! Born on this day in Beth-le-hem town is Christ the Lord, Christ the Lord.

1 Hark to the angels from heaven calling:
  "Shepherds wake, shepherds wake!
  Born on this day in Bethlehem town is
  Christ the Lord, Christ the Lord.

2 Hear, all ye shepherds in fields abiding,
  Leave your sheep, leave your sheep!
  Go to the manger, kneel thou before Him,
  Christ the Son, Christ the Son.

3 There shall ye find Him, in cradle lowly.
  Gloria, Gloria!
  O'er Her bless'd Son sweet Mary is watching.
  Christ is born, Christ is born!"

A Hungarian Christmas carol, *Menyböl as angyal*,
translated by Ruth Heller.

34. A POLISH TUNE

A traditional Polish carol, *Wśród nocnej ciszy*.

35. A CHRISTMAS SONG

Peacefully flowing

VOICES

PIANO

pp

with pedal

1. Winds through the o - live trees soft - ly did blow____ Round lit - tle Beth - le - hem long, long a - go. Sheep on the hill - side lay white as the snow,____ Shep-herds were watch-ing them long, long a - go.

L.H. (*sim.*)

A traditional Gascon carol.

8va bassa

1 Winds through the olive trees softly did blow
   Round little Bethlehem long, long ago.
   Sheep on the hillside lay white as the snow,
   Shepherds were watching them long, long ago.

2 Then from the happy skies angels bent low
   Singing their songs of joy long, long ago.
   For in His manger bed cradled we know
   Christ came to Bethlehem long, long ago.

36. SHEPHERDS, SHAKE OFF YOUR DROWSY SLEEP

1 Shepherds, shake off your drowsy sleep,
  Rise and leave your silly sheep;
  Angels from heaven all are singing,
  Tidings of great joy are bringing.
      Shepherds! the chorus come and swell!
      Sing noël, noël, noël.

2 Hark! even now the bells ring round,
  Listen to their merry sound;
  Hark! how the birds new songs are making,
  As if winter's chains were breaking.
      Shepherds! etc.

3 Cometh at length the age of peace,
  Strife and sorrow now shall cease;
  Prophets foretold the wondrous story
  Of this heaven-born Prince of Glory.
      Shepherds! etc.

4 Shepherds! then up and quick away,
  Seek the Babe ere break of day;
  He is the hope of every nation,
  All in Him shall find salvation.
      Shepherds! etc.

A traditional Besançon carol.

37. PATAPAN

Quick and merry
(last time CODA)

VOICES

1. Wil - lie, take your lit - tle drum, With your whi - stle,

RECORDERS

SMALL DRUM
or
WOOD BLOCK

Ro - bin, come! When we hear the fife and drum, *Tu - re - lu - re -*

- lu, pa - ta - pa - tan, When we hear the fife and drum, Christ-mas should be____

CODA

fro - lic - some.

repeat ad lib.,
dying away to nothing

1 Willie, take your little drum,
  With your whistle, Robin, come!
      When we hear the fife and drum,
  Ture-lure-lu, pata-pata-pan,
      When we hear the fife and drum,
      Christmas should be frolicsome.

2 Thus the man of olden days
  Loved the King of Kings to praise:
      When they hear the fife and drum,
  Ture-lure-lu, pata-pata-pan,
      When they hear the fife and drum,
      Sure our children won't be dumb!

3 God and man are now become
  More at one than fife and drum,
      When you hear the fife and drum,
  Ture-lure-lu, pata-pata-pan,
      When you hear the fife and drum,
      Dance, and make the village hum!

A Burgundian carol, from *Noëls Bourgignons de Bernard de la Monnoye*, 1842, translated by Percy Dearmer.

38. THE MOON SHINES BRIGHT

With movement, but not fast

VOICES

GUITAR
or
PIANO

1. The moon shines bright, and the stars_ give a light: A lit-tle be - fore it was day Our_ Lord, our_ God, He_ called on_ us, And. bid us a-wake_ and_ pray. 2. A -

CODA

1 The moon shines bright, and the stars give a light:
   A little before it was day
Our Lord, our God, He called on us,
   And bid us awake and pray.

2 Awake, awake, good people all;
   Awake, and you shall hear,
Our Lord, our God, died on the cross
   For us whom He loved so dear.

3 O fair, O fair Jerusalem,
   When shall I come to thee?
When shall my sorrows have an end,
   Thy joy that I may see?

4 The fields were green as green could be,
   When from His glorious seat
Our Lord, our God, He blessed us,
   With His heavenly dew so sweet.

5 And for the saving of our souls
   Christ died upon the cross;
We ne'er shall do for Jesus Christ
   As He has done for us.

6 The life of man is but a span,
   And cut down in its flower;
We are here today and tomorrow are gone,
   The creatures of an hour.

7 My song is done, I must be gone,
   I can stay no longer here.
God bless you all, both great and small,
   And send you a happy New Year.

Words and melody traditional.

39. TOMORROW SHALL BE MY DANCING DAY

Quick and rhythmic

VOICES

1. To - mor - row shall be ____ my danc - ing day: I would my true ____ love did ____ so

PIANO

f stacc. (as ²⁄₄) *sim.*

chance To ____ see the le - gend of ____ my play, To

call my true ____ love to ____ my dance: *Sing O my* ____

with pedal

1 Tomorrow shall be my dancing day:
   I would my true love did so chance
To see the legend of my play,
   To call my true love to my dance:
      Sing O my love, O my love, my love, my love;
   This have I done for my true love.

2 Then was I born of a virgin pure,
   Of her I took fleshly substance;
Thus was I knit to man's nature,
   To call my true love to my dance:
      Sing O my love, etc.

3 In a manger laid and wrapped I was,
   So very poor, this was my chance,
Betwixt an ox and a silly poor ass,
   To call my true love to my dance:
      Sing O my love, etc.

4 Then afterwards baptized I was;
   The Holy Ghost on me did glance,
My Father's voice heard from above,
   To call my true love to my dance:
      Sing O my love, etc.

Words and melody from Sandys' *Christmas Carols*, 1833. The text seems to go back earlier than the seventeenth century.

40. WASSAIL, WASSAIL, ALL OVER THE TOWN

1. Was - sail, was - sail,_ all o - ver the town! Our toast it is white, and our ale_ it_ is brown, Our bowl it_ is_ made of the white ma-ple tree; With the was - sail-ing bowl we'll drink_ to thee._____

2. So

1 Wassail, wassail, all over the town!
  Our toast it is white, and our ale it is brown,
  Our bowl it is made of the white maple tree;
  With the wassailing bowl we'll drink to thee.

2 So here is to Cherry and to his right cheek,
  Pray God send our master a good piece of beef,
  And a good piece of beef that may we all see;
  With the wassailing bowl we'll drink to thee.

3 And here is to Dobbin and to his right eye,
  Pray God send our master a good Christmas pie,
  And a good Christmas pie that may we all see;
  With our wassailing bowl we'll drink to thee.

4 So here is to Broad May and to her broad horn,
  May God send our master a good crop of corn,
  And a good crop of corn that may we all see;
  With the wassailing bowl we'll drink to thee.

5 And here is to Fillpail and to her left ear,
  Pray God send our master a happy New Year,
  And a happy New Year as e'er he did see;
  With our wassailing bowl we'll drink to thee.

6 And here is to Colly and to her long tail,
  Pray God send our master he never may fail
  A bowl of strong beer; I pray you draw near,
  And our jolly wassail it's then you shall hear.

7 Come, butler, come fill us a bowl of the best,
  Then we hope that your soul in heaven may rest;
  But if you do draw us a bowl of the small,
  Then down shall go butler, bowl and all.

8 Then here's to the maid in the lily white smock,
  Who tripped to the door and slipped back the lock!
  Who tripped to the door and pulled back the pin,
  For to let these jolly wassailers in.

Melody collected by R. Vaughan Williams.
Words traditional, collated by Percy Dearmer.

41. IN DULCI JUBILO

1. *In dulci jubilo*
   Let us our homage show;
   Our hearts' joy reclineth
   In præsepio,
   And like a bright star shineth
   Matris in gremio
   Alpha es et O!

2. *O Jesu parvule!*
   My heart is sore for Thee!
   Hear me, I beseech Thee,
   O Puer optime!
   My prayer let it reach Thee,
   O Princeps Gloriæ!
   Trache me post Te!

3. *O Patris caritas!*
   O Nati lenitas!
   Deeply were we stained
   Per nostra crimina;
   But Thou hast for us gained
   Cælorum gaudia:-
   O that we were there!

4. *Ubi sunt gaudia,*
   If that they be not there?
   There are angels singing
   Nova cantica;
   There the bells are ringing
   In Regis curia:
   O that we were there!

Translated from the German by R. L. de Pearsall.

42. ANGELS AND SHEPHERDS

1. Come all ye shep-herds and hark to our song! Come all ye shep-herds, Christ Je-sus is born! Lo, un-to us this day there is gi-ven Our Lord, Christ Je-sus, sent down from hea-ven!

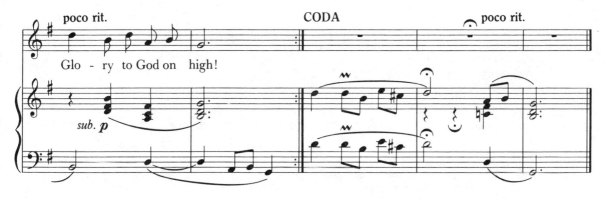

Glo - ry to God on high!

1 Come all ye shepherds and hark to our song!
Come all ye shepherds, Christ Jesus is born!
Lo, unto us this day there is given
Our Lord, Christ Jesus, sent down from heaven!
Glory to God on high!

2 Come all ye shepherds arise, leave your sheep!
Come to the stable Lord Jesus to seek.
Lo, in a manger lies Christ anointed
Whom, as our Saviour, God has appointed.
Glory to God on high!

3 Now join we the shepherds who to Bethlehem go.
Grant we, like them, Love's redemption will know.
Come and adore Him, He our Lord Jesus;
He now, the Word, in flesh dwells among us.
Glory to God on high!

A Czech carol, translated by Ruth Heller.

43. DECK THE HALL

1 Deck the hall with boughs of holly,
   Fa la la la la, la la la la.
'Tis the season to be jolly,
   Fa la la la la, la la la la.
Don we now our gay apparel,
   Fa la, la la, la la la,
Troll the ancient Yule-tide carol,
   Fa la la la la, la la la la.

2 See the blazing Yule before us,
   Fa la la la la, la la la la.
Strike the harp and join the chorus,
   Fa la la la la, la la la la.
Follow me in merry measure,
   Fa la, la la, la la la,
While I tell of Yule-tide treasure,
   Fa la la la la, la la la la.

3 Fast away the old year passes,
   Fa la la la la, la la la la.
Hail the new, ye lads and lasses,
   Fa la la la la, la la la la.
Sing we joyous all together,
   Fa la, la la, la la la,
Heedless of the wind and weather,
   Fa la la la la, la la la la.

A traditional Welsh carol.

44. THE BOYS' CAROL

(Personent Hodie)

In the time of a march

VOICES

PIANO

ff

(always percussive: without pedal throughout)

1. Per - so - nent ho - di - e Vo - ces pu - er - u - læ,
1. Sing a - loud on this day! Child - ren all raise the lay.

mf

always staccato

Lau - dan - tes jo - cun - de Qui no - bis est na - tus,
Cheer - ful - ly we and they Hast - en to a - dore Thee,

Sum - mo De - o da - tus, Et de vir-, vir-, vir-,
Sent from high - est glo - ry, *For us born, born, born,*

dim. *p*

Et de vir-, vir-, vir-, Et de vir - gi - ne - o
For us born, born, born, *For us born on this morn*

cresc.

from 𝄋

ven - tre pro - cre - a - tus.
Of the Vir - gin Ma - ry.

(last time to CODA)

ff

CODA

dim. poco a poco *pp*

1 Personent hodie
  Voces puerulæ,
  Laudantes jocunde
  Qui nobis est natus,
  Summo Deo datus,
  Et de vir-, vir-, vir-,
  Et de vir-, vir-, vir-,
  Et de virgineo ventre procreatus.

1 *Sing aloud on this day!*
  Children all raise the lay.
  Cheerfully we and they
  Hasten to adore Thee,
  Sent from highest glory,
  For us born, born, born,
  For us born, born, born,
  For us born on this morn
  Of the Virgin Mary.

2 In mundo nascitur,
  Pannis involvitur,
  Præsepi ponitur
  Stabulo brutorum,
  Rector supernorum.
  Perdidit, -dit, -dit,
  Perdidit, -dit, -dit,
  Perdidit spolia princeps infernorum.

2 *Now a child He is born,*
  Swathing bands Him adorn,
  Manger bed He'll not scorn,
  Ox and ass are near Him;
  We as Lord revere Him,
  And the vain, vain, vain,
  And the vain, vain, vain,
  And the vain powers of hell
  Spoiled of prey now fear Him.

3 Magi tres venerunt,
  Parvulum inquirunt,
  Parvulum inquirunt,
  Stellulam sequendo,
  Ipsum adorando,
  Aurum, thus, thus, thus,
  Aurum, thus, thus, thus,
  Aurum, thus, et myrrham ei offerendo.

3 *From the far Orient*
  Guiding star wise men sent;
  Him to seek their intent,
  Lord of all creation;
  Kneel in adoration.
  Gifts of gold, gold, gold,
  Gifts of gold, gold, gold,
  Gifts of gold, frankincense,
  Myrrh for their oblation.

4 Omnes clericuli,
  Pariter pueri,
  Cantent ut angeli:
  Advenisti mundo,
  Laudes tibi fundo.
  Ideo, -o, -o,
  Ideo, -o, -o,
  Ideo gloria in excelsis Deo!

4 *All must join Him to praise;*
  Men and boys voices raise
  On this day of all days;
  Angel voices ringing,
  Christmas tidings bringing.
  Join we all, all, all,
  Join we all, all, all,
  Join we all, 'Gloria
  In excelsis' singing.

From *Piae Cantiones*, 1582. Translation by John A. Parkinson, reprinted by permission of Oxford University Press.

45. SLEEP, MY SAVIOUR, SLEEP

★The 2nd part may be sung by another voice or played on recorders. The pause in the final bar applies to v. 2 only.

1 Sleep, my Saviour, sleep
On Thy bed of hay,
Ere the morning angel cometh
To the moonlit olive gardens
Wiping tears away.

2 Sleep, my Saviour, sleep
Sweet on Mary's breast,
Now the shepherds kneel adoring,
Now the mother's heart is joyous.
Have a happy rest.

A Czech carol. English version by S. Baring-Gould.

46. WITHIN A HUMBLE STABLE

Lively, but not too fast

VOICES

PIANO

f

1. With -
(last time to CODA)

-in a hum-ble sta - ble Not far from Beth - le - hem,___ With

cresc.   *dim.*

nei - ther mink nor sa - ble Nor crown nor di - a - dem,___ He

cresc.   *dim.*

sleeps in cra-dle of straw And for His cour - tiers, swains and cat - tle. The

lightly

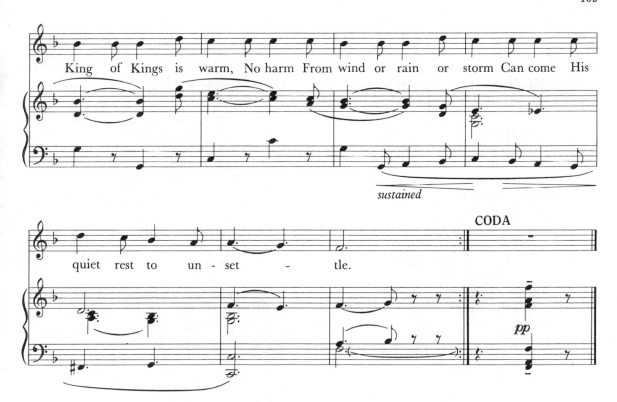

King of Kings is warm, No harm From wind or rain or storm Can come His

sustained

CODA

quiet rest to un - set - tle.

pp

1 Within a humble stable
  Not far from Bethlehem,
  With neither mink nor sable
  Nor crown nor diadem,
  He sleeps in cradle of straw
      And for
  His courtiers, swains and cattle.
  The King of Kings is warm,
      No harm
  From wind or rain or storm
      Can come
  His quiet rest to unsettle.

2 Beside him is his mother
  With father Joseph near.
  There is not any other
  His poverty to share.
  But ox and asses wait
      To greet
  All Christians at the stable.
  So hasten to the King
      And bring
  Your joyful hearts and sing
      To Him
  The best that you are able.

3 His Grace the Lord Archbishop
Will head the happy throng,
And after him his canons
In vestments fine and long.
Their linen rochets laced
    With taste
And purple cassocks flowing,
They'll lead the peoples' praise
    And raise
Their voices in gay
    Roundelays,
Their love for Jesus showing.

4 The learnèd judges follow
In scarlet robes arrayed,
Their sleeves all trimmed with ermine
And whitest wigs displayed.
The university don
    Comes then
The Chancellor and professors.
Their gowns of black and hoods
    Look good
And make us feel we should
    And could
Of learning be possessors.

5 Next come the country mayors
In fur-trimmed civic dress,
Their mayoral chains all shining
As slowly they process.
The bankers follow and hold
    Their gold
As offerings for the King.
And silver coins that gleam
    And seem
Like stars of heavenly sheen
    That beam
Their brightness over everything.

6 And now the townsfolk follow,
All craftsmen in their trades,
In simple workmen's clothing,
No silks or rich brocades.
They bring their finest arts
    With hearts
So thankful and so gay.
Their wives bring homespun shawls
    And all
The children big or small
    A ball
Or simple toy for Jesu's play.

7 But best of all the presents
That Jesus can receive
Is contrite hearts and spirits
That earnestly believe
In Christ, the Lord of Lords,
    Whose word
Gives comfort to the sinner.
So try with all your might
    To fight
Old Satan's wiles this
    Christmas night
And you will be the winner.

A Besançon Noël, *Dessu un pou de peille*, translated by F.J.S.

47. PUER NATUS

Chorale harmonized
by J. S. Bach

S. A.

1. A boy was born in Beth - le - hem,

T. B.

In Beth - - le - hem, Re - joice for that, Je - ru - sa - lem!

v. 5 And glo - - ry bright,

Al - le - lu - ya, Al - le - - - lu - ya.

1 A boy was born in Bethlehem,
   In Bethlehem,
  Rejoice for that, Jerusalem!
   Alleluya, Alleluya.

2 For low He lay within a stall,
   Within a stall,
  Who rules for ever over all;
   Alleluya, Alleluya.

3 He let Himself a servant be,
   A servant be,
  That all mankind He might set free:
   Alleluya, Alleluya.

4 Then praise the Word of God who came,
   The Word of God who came,
  To dwell within a human frame,
   Alleluya, Alleluya.

5 And praised be God in threefold might,
   And glory bright,
  Eternal, good, and infinite.
   Alleluya, Alleluya.

Traditional German, 16th century. Words translated by Percy Dearmer.

48. TO THE TOWN OF BETHLEHEM

1. To the town of Beth - le - hem some shep - herds came,

Leav - ing their flocks to wor - ship Christ the King;

Through earth and air their prais - es loud - ly ring - ing,

1 To the town of Bethlehem some shepherds came,
  Leaving their flocks to worship Christ the King;
  Through earth and air their praises loudly ringing,
  Shepherds sing, shepherds sing.

2 Graciously the Infant Jesus smiled at them,
  Gladness and joy their simple hearts did fill;
  Glory to God in heaven, Glory to God in heaven,
  Peace to men of goodwill.

A traditional Polish carol, translated by C.F.

114

49. THE COVENTRY CAROL

(Original Version)

Lul - ly, lul - la, thou lit - tle ti - ny child, By by, lul -

Lul - ly, lul - la, thou lit - tle ti - ny child, By by, lul -

Lul - ly, lul - la, thou lit - tle ti - ny child, By by, lul -

-ly lul - lay, thou lit - tle ti - ny child, By by, lul - ly lul - lay.

-ly lul - lay, thou lit - tle ti - ny child, By by, lul - ly lul - lay.

-ly lul - lay, thou lit - tle ti - ny child, By by, lul - ly lul - lay.

Lully, lulla, thou little tiny child,
By by, lully lullay.

1 O sisters too,
How may we do
  For to preserve this day
This poor youngling
For whom we do sing,
  By by, lully lullay?

2 Herod, the king,
In his raging,
  Charged he hath this day
His men of might,
In his own sight,
  All young children to slay.

3 That woe is me,
Poor child for thee!
  And ever morn and day,
For thy parting
Neither say nor sing
  By by, lully lullay!

The text is that of Robert Croo, 1534, reprinted by E. Rhys in *Everyman and other Plays*. The tune was discovered and printed by Thomas Sharp, in *Dissertations*, 1825.

50. MUMMERS' SONG

A traditional Hampshire carol.

INDEX OF TITLES

INDEX OF FIRST LINES